P9-CBR-624

shooting

Ri

star

der

NAYOUNG JIN
GENEVIÈVE CÔTÉ

To my friend Ellinor Crux
and my grandpa Yong Tak Lee,
with love and appreciation
for being who they are.
—*N.J.*

For my sister
Marie-Luce,
with love.
—*G.C.*

Published in 2017 by Simply Read Books
www.simplyreadbooks.com
Text © 2017 Nayoung Jin
Illustrations © 2017 Geneviève Côté

All rights reserved. No part of this publication may be reproduced,
stored in a retrieval system, or transmitted, in any form or by any
means, electronic, mechanical, photocopying, recording or otherwise,
without the written permission of the publisher. The publisher does
not have any control over and does not assume any responsibility
for author or third-party websites or their content.

LIBRARY AND ARCHIVES CANADA CATALOGUING IN PUBLICATION

Jin, Nayoung, author
Shooting star rider / written by Nayoung Jin ; illustrated
by Geneviève Côté.

ISBN 978-1-77229-020-2 (hardback)

I. Côté, Geneviève, 1964-, illustrator II. Title.

PZ7.1.J56Sho 2016   jC813'.6   C2016-907205-3

We gratefully acknowledge for their financial support of our
publishing program the Canada Council for the Arts,
the BC Arts Council, and the Government of Canada
through the Canada Book Fund (CBF).

Manufactured in Korea
Book design by Heather Lohnes
10 9 8 7 6 5 4 3 2 1

shooting star
Rider

written by
NAYOUNG JIN

illustrated by
GENEVIÈVE CÔTÉ

SIMPLY READ BOOKS

ONE WARM SUMMER NIGHT, a shooting star swept across the sky.

Elinor looked out her window and made a wish:

"Make Grandpa well."

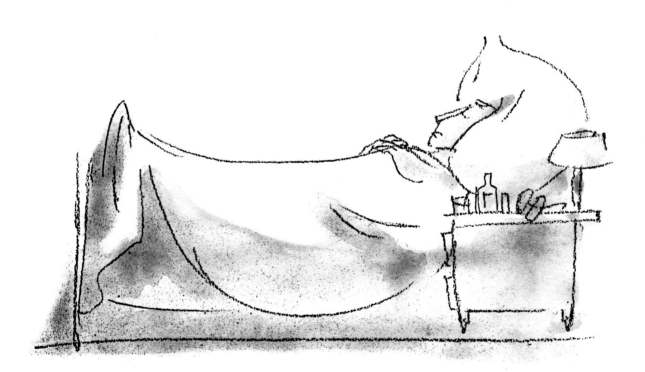

She waited.
And waited.

And waited.

Then, one morning,
Elinor found a
postcard on her
windowsill.

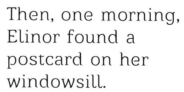

It read:

Dear Shooting Star Wisher on Earth.
Please don't wait for miracles from
shooting stars anymore.
Sincerely,
 A Shooting Star

"How could this be?"
shouted Elinor.

She wasn't ready to give up.
Elinor ran to the beach
with a kite...

...and flew up to the sky,

then into outer space,

passing by the moon.

"Who wrote this horrible postcard?" Elinor asked, holding it up.

The stars were silent.

"Who wrote this?" she said again.

The stars looked nervous and concerned. They whispered, mumbled and murmered amongst themselves.

Then they pointed far behind them at a big star, much larger than the rest.

The star was sitting alone, busily writing something. All around it, postcards floated and twirled.

"You mustn't stop people from dreaming, from wishing," said Elinor, holding up her postcard.

The big star said, "There are so many wishes! So little time!"

"But there are so many of you!" said Elinor.

"Yes, but we have to work very hard,"
said the big star, "lighting up the sky
for the people on Earth. We are the
lighthouses for spaceships."

"Oh," said Elinor.

"And we help lost travelers find their
way home. To faraway planets."

"Oh," said Elinor. "Then no more
wishes? Absolutely none?"

"People can do without wishes! If you
want to gain something, you work hard
for it. And you musn't be so greedy."

Elinor thought about her sick grandpa and shook her head. "You don't understand. Come with me. I'll show you."

"Me? I'm a very busy star," said the big star, waving a magic wand.

"If you don't come now, I'll get all the
star-wishers from Earth and you'll have
to answer them right here."

"Oh no!"

"So, shall we?"

"Well...okay, dear, you've got ten
minutes with me."

So Elinor left for Earth
riding a sea of shooting stars,
the big star gliding behind.

First, they visited a boy and his mama with a second-hand violin. The boy put the violin in his case, quickly closed the lid and said, "All I need in life is right here!"

His mama sighed.

"Free violin lessons," she whispered her wish.

Next, a boy living with his parents
who were always arguing.

"Wish we could all laugh
ourselves silly instead,"
he said.

Finally,
a woman.

"Please help find our dog, Lui.
We lost him at the mountain.
Bring him home, please..."

"Oh...oh," said the shooting stars, blinking their eyes.

"See? I told you," said Elinor.

Just as they were leaving, Elinor said, "Look!"

Everyone watched a girl in the park who no longer blew away dandelion seeds, or tried to find four-leaf clovers, or ran to catch a feather flying in the air...

The girl burst into tears.

The big star asked, "Why is she so upset?"

But nobody knew because the girl hadn't made a single wish.

"Things have to change!" the big star said, as the little stars listened seriously.

"Goodnight, Elinor. Sweet dreams,"
wished the big and little shooting stars.

The next morning, Elinor found her grandpa in the garden picking apricots.

"Are you feeling better?" she asked.

"I'm having a good day," said Grandpa. "I thought I would make you some of my famous apricot dumplings."

Even though Elinor couldn't see the stars,
she knew they were up there.

"Thank you, shooting stars,"
she said.

The
end.

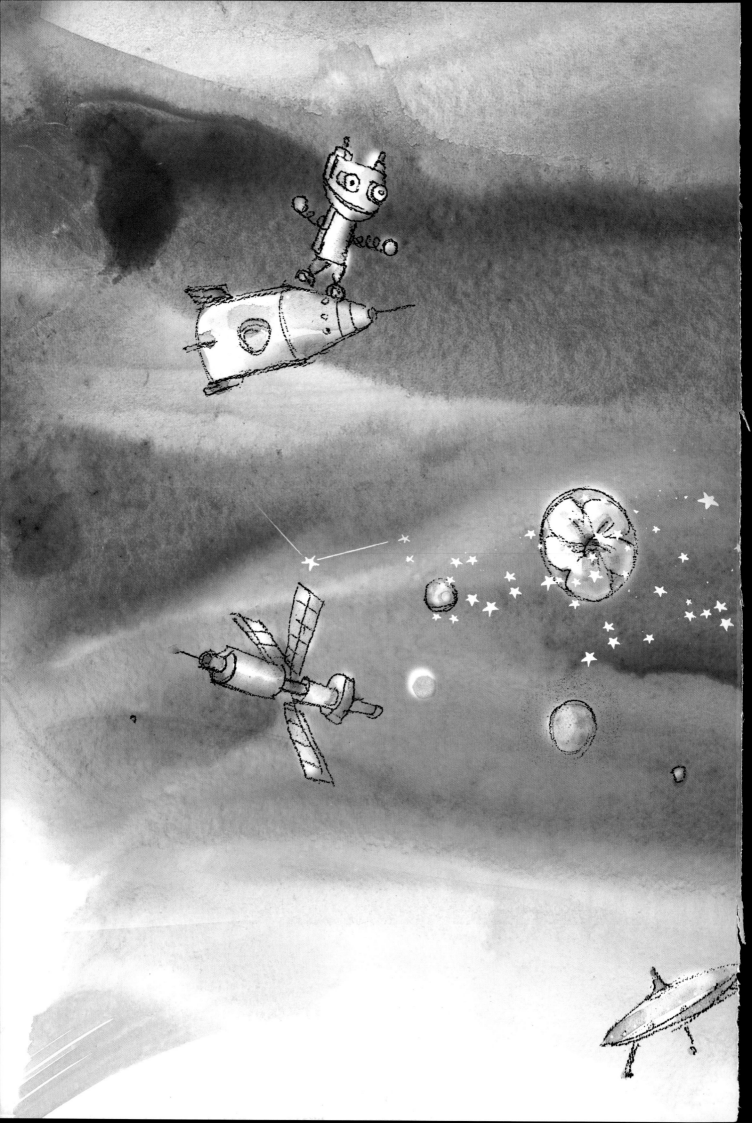